Finding A Friend

By
Zilpha Booth

A Windswept Book
Windwept House — Mt. Desert, Maine

Library of Congress Catalog Number 86-050987

ISBN 0 932 433-22-7

Printed in the United States of America
For the Publisher by
Downeast Graphics and Printing, Inc.
Ellsworth, Maine

This book is dedicated
to my grandchildren

"Hey, Dad, here comes the truck," shouted Andy Green. He jumped up and down with excitement. His blue eyes sparkled. Andy was anxious to see the boy who was riding in the truck.

Andy watched his father greet Mr. Stuart, who was to be the new supervisor in the orchard. Andy's father owned a big apple orchard. Many people worked for him, caring for the trees, picking and packing the apples. Mr. Stuart was to be in charge of the workers. He and his family would live in a little house near the orchard. Andy was waiting to see the Stuart's son Mike, who was eight, just his age. Andy liked living near the orchard out in the country, but he was lonely for a real special friend... perhaps it would be Mike.

Out of the corner of his eye Andy watched Mike Stuart slowly climb down from his father's truck.

Mike was looking at Andy carefully, too. He was waiting to see what Andy would do. Sometimes kids laughed at him. Sometimes they yelled at him and wouldn't let him play with them. Mike was shy and feeling a bit scared as he looked to see what this new boy would do.

Just then Andy smiled at him and a big grin spread across Mike's face. Maybe this boy would play with him. Maybe he would even be a friend.

Andy shouted, "Come on, let's go swing," and he ran toward the swings hanging from the big tree. Mike followed with a shuffling, quick walk. As their parents watched, the boys swung and laughed together. Later Andy took Mike indoors and showed him his room, his books and his toys. They had fun, but something about Mike bothered Andy.

That night after dinner he asked his mother, "What's the matter with Mike, Mom? You said he was eight years old like me, but he talks like a little kid. He can't even run properly. He can't play my games."

"Mike *is* eight years old, Andy, but he is retarded, so he acts younger."

"What's retarded, and how'd he get retarded?" Andy wasn't sure what his mother meant.

His mother replied, "Sometimes when a baby first starts to grow inside the mother, one of the tiny cells doesn't develop in the right way. This makes a difference as the baby forms and grows, and the brain area is affected. We call such a child retarded. He won't be able to think as quickly as most children and he will be slow to learn. Also, he may look slightly different. He may have slanted eyes and a squashed looking nose as Mike does. Being retarded is no one's fault. It is a sad thing that sometimes happens."

Andy thought of all the things his mother said. Then he spoke slowly. "Mike can't read either."

"That's right, Andy," replied his father. "Mike will learn to read, but never as well as you do. He won't be able to run as fast either. But there are lots of things he can do and he is a very friendly boy. I think you two will have fun playing together."

Andy and Mike did play together often. They each had a red wagon and they pretended the wagons were delivery trucks. Sometimes Andy's mother would ask, "Will you ride in your trucks and deliver a message to Dad?" Or she'd ask, "Will you take some lemonade to your fathers in the orchard?" With great chugging and roaring noises the boys would start their trucks and be off to the orchard.

Near the orchard was a blueberry field and Andy and Mike had been waiting for the little green berries to turn blue. One morning Andy rode his bike down the hill to Mike's house, shouting, "Hey, Mike, the blueberries are ripe! The blueberries are ripe! Mom says if we pick some, she'll make us blueberry pancakes for lunch."

Mike smiled a big happy smile. When he had seen Andy on his bike, he had thought that Andy was going bike riding with the other boys. Mike felt lonesome when this happened because he couldn't go.

But Andy was calling, "Come on, Mike, get your pail. Let's go blueberrying."

Mike quickly found his little blueberry picking pail and followed Andy into the field. Swinging their pails the boys wandered among the low blueberry bushes.

"Only take the blue ones, Mike," warned Andy. The berries made a little plunk, plunk sound as they were dropped into the pails.

In a little while Andy began to eat berries instead of putting them in his pail. He looked at Mike to see if he was watching but Mike was eating berries too. Andy laughed.

"They're good, aren't they?" he asked. Mike shook his head yes.

Sitting quietly and popping berries into their mouths, they heard a rustle behind them. Looking around they saw a small brown rabbit hop along the path. Andy motioned for Mike to be still. The little bunny wiggled its nose and sniffed at the grass. Then the rabbit's big ears twitched and he lifted up his head. Seeing the boys he hopped away as fast as he could. The boys laughed to see the little white tail bobbing up and down.

"We'd better put some more berries in our pails if we want Mom to make blueberry pancakes," said Andy.

"I like blueberry pancakes," replied Mike.

There was no talking as the boys began picking again, and soon their pails were half full.

Mike put his pail on the ground by a rock to tie his sneaker. When he started to pick up the pail, he saw something green and shiny beside it.

"Andy, look!" he called. "A snake!"

"Where? Where?" asked Andy.

"In the bushes!" shouted Mike.

The boys scrambled in the grass trying to catch the slender green snake, but he was too quick for them and slithered away under a stone.

"Let's see if we can find him again", said Andy.

The boys poked all around the bushes but they didn't see the snake again.

"I guess we'd better go home now and see if Mom is ready to make blueberry pancakes for our lunch," said Andy.

The boys walked home chanting, "Blueberry pancakes for lunch. Blueberry pancakes for lunch!"

Andy and Mike took swimming lessons at the nearby lake. Both boys enjoyed their swim days. Andy had taken lessons before and could swim under water. Mike was just beginning to learn. The teacher was pleased with them both. Usually, after the lessons Mike and Andy had happy, smiling faces.

One day, however, as Mrs. Green drove Andy and Mike home after their swimming lesson, she knew something was wrong. Andy was sitting very still, staring out the window with his back turned toward Mike. Mike was pounding his fist on his knee. He always did this when something was troubling him. Both boys had sad, unhappy faces. Mrs. Green wondered what had happened at the swimming lesson.

At lunch, Andy stopped eating and said, "I don't want to take anymore swimming lessons."

"Why, Andy?" asked his mother.

"Because Mike always messes things up," Andy scowled.

"What do you mean? How does Mike mess things up?"

"Well, today at the end of the lesson, when we were allowed to play with the beach ball, he wouldn't take turns. He just grabbed the ball and held on to it. He had one of his stubborn spells and he wouldn't let anyone play with it. The boys yelled, 'You dumb kid, let us have the ball.' "

"I tried to get Mike to give me the ball, but he ran away with it and he cried. Joe yelled at me, 'You're as dumb as Mike if you're his friend. You're retarded, too.' Mom, why can't Mike be like other kids?"

"I wish he could be, Andy, but he isn't. It's sad. Mike is usually such a friendly, happy boy, but sometimes he gets upset because he can't do all the things other boys can. And the other boys don't understand Mike the way you do."

After Andy finished lunch he said, "I'm going to see if Mike wants to go for a walk. I guess it's hard for him to understand things."

"Mike's lucky he has you for a friend." Mrs. Green gave Andy a little hug. "I know it's hard for you sometimes, but boys like Mike need a friend more than other boys do."

The great secret began on a morning when Andy and Mike went to watch Mr. Green spraying the apples in the south orchard. The small apples had to be sprayed so that scab and rust spots wouldn't spoil them. Andy's father was driving the tractor.

The boys watched for a while and then went off to explore the huge boulders at the side of the field. There were rocks jumbled every which way and a great tangle of bushes. Suddenly, Mike disappeared.

"Andy! Andy!"

Andy heard his friend's frightened voice. It seemed to be coming from underneath the rocks and bushes! Quickly Andy pushed aside branches and leaves and then he found the hole between the rocks, and slipped down beside Mike.

"Hey, look what you found! I never knew there was a cave here."

The cave was cool, with some sunshiny light coming through the opening. It was very quiet and peaceful.

For a while the boys just sat very still, looking around.

"This is a great cave," Andy said, grinning at Mike.

Mike smiled back. "Great cave." He grabbed Andy's hand and together they crawled all around the cave.

"Let's make this our secret, Mike," said Andy. "Don't tell anyone." Did Mike understand what a 'secret' was?

As they walked home Andy kept repeating, "It's a secret. Don't tell." Mike grinned a big grin and nodded his head.

"Secret!" he said.

After that there were many days when the boys ran down to the cave. When they were allowed to take their lunches to the south orchard they would slip into the cool, quiet cave and eat their favorite peanut butter and jelly sandwiches.

"Nobody knows where we are!"

Then they would grin at each other, feeling secret and important.

Sometimes Mike had to go to the doctor for a checkup. One day as he and his mother were coming home, she had to drive really slowly because it was so foggy that she could hardly see the road. As they entered their driveway they saw Mike's Dad and Mr. and Mrs. Green and some of the men who worked in the orchard all standing together talking intently and looking worried.

"What's the trouble?" Mrs. Stuart asked Mrs. Green.

"Andy's lost! He said he was taking his lunch to eat with his father in the south orchard, but his Dad hasn't seen him all day. We don't know where he is. He's never been away this long. We don't know where to look, and it's so foggy!"

Mike didn't understand all they said, but he knew everyone was worried. He heard the words, "Andy", "south orchard" and "lunch". He sat very still and quiet. He was thinking, "Where's Andy?" He gently pounded his fist on his knee, showing that something puzzled him. And then suddenly he knew. His hand was still. He looked around. No one was watching him. Andy had said, "Secret, don't tell."

Mike slipped away from the talking people.

That noon, instead of going to meet his father, Andy had decided to check the cave. The heavy fog made the rocks very slippery. As he climbed down over the big, wet boulders, he fell, *hard*, on to the tumbled rocks on the floor of the cave.

"Ouch!" he cried. His leg was crumpled under him. He couldn't move it. Was it broken? There was no one to help. No one who knew where he was. No one even knew about the cave except Mike, and Mike had gone to the doctor.

Andy cried for a little while, and then he tried shouting, "Help, somebody, help!"

That didn't help, either, and by then the pain in his leg was so bad it made him feel sick and groggy. Andy fell asleep.

Andy woke up suddenly, frightened. There had been a noise. He knew he was in the cave, but the thick fog made everything scary. It was darker, almost night, and his leg hurt more than ever. He heard the noise again. Something was pushing through the bushes into the cave. It was hard to see, but then he recognized Mike's head.

"Oh, Mike, I'm here," he shouted. "Mike! I'm glad it's you."

Mike stumbled over the rocks to his friend.

"Andy, Andy." Mike grinned as he patted Andy's leg.

"Ouch! Don't!"

"Andy, what's the matter?" asked Mike.

"Mike, go tell my father I've hurt my leg."

"Come on," said Mike, trying to lift Andy up. "Come with me."

"No, Mike, go tell my father. Tell him I'm in the secret cave."

"SECRET, Andy?"

"It's not a secret now, Mike, just go as fast as you can. It's not a secret anymore. Bring Dad and your father here."

Mike stared at Andy, wagging his head and pounding his fist on his knee. "Not secret?"

Then he climbed out of the cave. "Not secret," he repeated. Andy heard him thrashing away through the bushes.

Would Mike really be able to get help? Andy thought Mike wanted to help him, but it was hard to know when Mike understood things. Andy remembered his father saying that Mike was a very friendly boy. And they *were* friends... and friends always helped each other...

Mike found his father with Mr. Green and some of the men. They were starting to search the woods. He pulled his father's jacket.

"Mike, I'm busy now. Go into the house," his father said.

"Andy!" said Mike.

"Yes, Mike, I'm going to look for Andy."

"Andy in cave. Not secret."

"Secret? What! What are you saying, Mike? Do you know where Andy is?" Mr. Stuart looked at Mike. Mike nodded and grinned and pulled his father's jacket again.

"Cave. Andy. *Come!*"

"All right, son. I guess you really know where he is. Show me where Andy is."

The men followed Mike to the cave. Everyone was happy when they found Andy there. Mr. Green carried Andy home and took him to the doctor. His leg was broken and he had to have a cast put on it, but the doctor assured him that it would soon be as good as ever.

A few days later, as the Stuarts and the Greens sat together at a picnic supper on the porch, Mr. Green said, "I had forgotten all about that old cave." Putting his arm around Mike he said, "You figured out where Andy was. We're proud of you, Mike. We're glad you're Andy's friend."

Andy grinned at Mike. "So am I."

About the Author

Zilpha Booth, the mother of a retarded son, has for many years been involved in activities related to mental retardation. Her aim is to create better understanding of life situations of the handicapped.

She and her husband live in Bar Harbor, Maine. They have three other children and four grandchildren.

Previously she has written short stories for children and a book about her son entitled MOMMY DON'T CRY.